HONEYCOMBED

ROBERT JOHN

Published and Manufactured by Softwood Books
EU Responsible person: Maddy Glenn
Office 2, Wharfside House, Prentice Road, Stowmarket, Suffolk, IP14 1RD
www.softwoodbooks.com
hello@softwoodbooks.com

EU Rep:
Authorised Rep Compliance Ltd., Ground Floor, 71 Lower Baggot Street, Dublin, D02 P593, Ireland
www.arccompliance.com
info@arccompliance.com

Paperback ISBN: 978-1-0369-0161-5

A COUPLE YEARS AGO

Prologue

When It Rains It Pours

Imagine if 18% of humans had a condition called 'Dermorhea'.

This is where the times at which people contract diarrhoea, the waste is not evacuated in the regular manner. Instead, it leaves the body evenly through every pore, oozing slowly throughout the day and night until it's all gone. It's pretty grim, but imagine the ramifications amongst all the cultures around the world. The inclusivity and outcasts. The care and persecution. The fear and appraisals.

Most places would insist that you avoid work if you were squitting through your skin. HR would certainly step in. Governments would probably advise lying in the bath all day under care.

Baths would be made to certain specifications that would filter and flush – more plush for the 1% of the 18%. Eyeball goggles and lip–mouth nostril covers with tubes attached to enable breathing and the consumption of food and drink, with attachments to connect and replace, and home deliveries dropping off top-ups.

Imagine Dermorhea a couple years ago and throughout our history, sending in the drugged-up naked shit walkers behind enemy lines to sabotage, demoralise, and confuse the enemy.

Powerful people like kings and warlords who insist on the touch of an unlucky lady regardless of their unpleasant affliction. The paintings and sculptures of the diseased, and poems. The many forums and secret secretion societies that arise and dissolve.

Sometimes a minority who've been used outside of their own volition can instil sympathy in the majority. This can happen passively or more assertively until the minority folds into the majority.

The Opener

Things take time.

Sometimes it's better to wait for the apple to sweeten,

Patience is a worthwhile pursuit,

Strength over time because if it's brittle, it's weakened,

Entropy is a worldwide absolute.

Everything is connected. Religion said it and science shows it.

Take everyone's eyes out and we all look the same.

Things take time.

Introduction

Our perception of things can seem correct until we see otherwise. New information can be welcomed with open arms. It can also cause us to throw up arms and even bear arms.

If we dig a little deeper, we may find what we're looking for. If we don't dig at all, we may discover a ceiling beneath our floor.

Welcome. My pseudonym is Jon White, a variation of my real name. I'm a 39-year-old man with a wife, a toddler daughter, and a teenage stepson. I have a family, I have friends, I have interests and curiosity. I see things widely, I do things tidily, and I want to see the real you. I want to see you see me as you. How can we not be the beings who I met in the raves? Destined for graves testing degrades like a pest in the waves – the best ones behave. The waves, with the lost and the brave at cost for the swathes like moths to the flames.

No, we're alright. Things are better than they've ever been. People are cleverer than they've ever been and we're doing things that are way beyond ancient kings. Drones, smart toilets, quantum computing, space soldiers, paper clips, and Netflix – those old kingy types had no idea.

There's a lot more that's possible now for the individual. Not all individuals benefit, and a lot who could benefit don't.

I'm an ex-soldier who lives a completely different life to the life I lived a couple years ago.

I took what I needed from it and moved on in the direction of further betterment and personal growth.

For legal and metalegal purposes, this book should be treated as fiction. See you at the final curtain, and maybe beyond.

PART ONE – MILITARY

Bangin' Sangin

Me, the 50-caliber gun, general-purpose machine gun, plus my own weapons were on the roof. There were optics to help me see further afield and at night, plus the standard SUSAT optics on my rifle. My field of view up there was 360°. There was some big open space to the front and right and some closer walls and walkways. A local graveyard was at the rear with scattered scars of projectiles. There was a slope to the left that got steeper at the end towards the burn pit. The roof was on an old school, abandoned and taken over. Occupied by us and others before. The ongoing wear and weight after rainfall forced a heavy section of the roof onto a marine's bed. If he was somewhere else at the moment it fell, he'd be saved.

What are the odds of that? The exact part of the roof that fell through first, and it happened to be over his bed. The odds had to be high.

Well, don't bet against the house then. He was on patrol at the time. I'm sure he's fine now.

Me and his marine mates helped him clear it. He saw the funny side, but he did come back to find his cot bed caved in by bulletproof mud. This was life at Patrol Base Tangiers near Sangin, Afghanistan. I did a winter tour. I flew over in the beginning of the first week in December 2008 and came back middle of April 2009.

The Taliban left a winter contingent whilst the main bulk of their group went away for R and R. The summers got hot.

We did eight 15-minute stints at each watch point in Tangiers. The roof was the last of the eight sentry positions before you were off duty for a few hours.

This was a couple years ago before they changed tactics and replaced warning shots with flares. It was nighttime and I heard digging. The only digging that happens at night is when IEDs are being planted in the ground. No more or less than two of them were at it. I couldn't see them, but they were close.

Maybe I shouldn't have fired.

The bullet landed in the general direction of where they were against a known solid target that caused no harm to anybody as per the rules of engagement, but it made them stop digging and leave.

The patrol found nothing the next day so they must have taken the device with them and used it for somewhere else. I felt like I should have let them dig it in, and the patrol would have found and destroyed it.

They were deterred from digging, and who knows what that means. Maybe this encounter pushed one of them over the edge to leave the area for good. Maybe he sabotaged other devices out of fear or rebellion. Maybe not though. How can we know if one outcome is better than the other? Like when I fired a shot at that boy.

I'm sure he's fine now as well. He was about 7 then so he'll be about 22 now in 2024. He probably has a wife and a child of his own. He did need a warning, though. It was very silly digging in the ground in the line of sight of us. A less scrupulous soldier could've got the wrong idea and justified the kill.

From the roof, I warned the men below who were gathering for a patrol that I'd be firing a warning shot. He was around 250 metres away, and I fired to the left of him as he casually dug away.

It landed at his feet, two feet to his right–my left, a lot closer than I intended. The dust kicked up, and he looked up. I gestured for him to go away, and he ran off to the right.

I later imagined him running to his friends and telling them that we fired at him. Then I imagined his dad asking him what he was doing, then his dad teaching him to avoid digging in the view of soldiers because of what it looks like.

I'm very grateful that the shot didn't fall any further to the right.

Parashooting Stars

The choice was a tandem freefall from around 30,000 feet or a static line jump from 4000 feet. I did want to do the freefall, and still do, but I wanted my first time to be by myself. I wanted to throw myself out of the plane instead of being strapped to someone else who throws me out.

The Silver Stars parachute display team were offering training for jumps, and I jumped at the chance. The two groups got split up and received separate training.

There were about twenty people in the static line group, and we underwent the mandatory and relatively small amount of training. We did a whole day of practising how to land and what to do if things go wrong, etc., then a refresher the next day, before packing our own chutes and getting airborne.

Some people were more nervous than others. I fed off their nervousness to a certain extent. I knew that I wouldn't panic and forget the drills, so I was confident moving forward.

This was a couple years ago when I was a young buck in the army, around 19 or 20 years old. Regardless of how I felt, we all reassured each other and made sure that we knew what we were doing. It was a normal thing for the stronger ones to help the less stronger ones through tough times. Some are tough sometimes, and others other times. Some are tough all the time, and others most of the time. I was tough this time.

The jump was in the afternoon. The weather was nearly perfect: minimal winds, mostly blue sky, and a mild temperature. The nervousness grew in the group as we got suited up and saw the plane that we'd be jumping from. It was a small blue-and-white thing that looked like a toy.

We squeezed into it and sat on the floor. There were no seats other than the one for the pilot and the one for the co-pilot.

We had to sit in two files of six with our legs wrapped around the person in front. There were two instructors with us, one by the door who would control the exit and one at the back for support.

The propellers spun, and we were airborne. After a short noisy flight, we got to the right altitude. One of the preparations on the ground from the previous day was to see how much we weigh. The heaviest jumps first and so on until the lightest. This was to prevent anyone from catching up and collapsing someone else's canopy who'd jumped out beforehand.

The instructor opened the thin door and told the first person to jump. Off he went, and it was my turn next. I shuffled to the door and sat with my legs dangling down as I waited for the thumbs up to jump. There was a noticeable delay before I was instructed to move back into the plane, then the door was closed. We had gone too far away from the drop zone, and the pilot wanted to make another pass to give us the best chance of landing in the designated drop zone area.

At this point, I looked back and noticed a couple of my mates looking uneasy. I made some jokes to lift their spirits and made my way back to the open door as instructed. I remember looking down at the fields and thinking that it's too far away to be scared of the height. I only had the emergency drills buzzing around my mind anyway. I thought that if anything went wrong,

I'd follow the training and it'll be fine. Trust the kit and trust the drills.

With my legs dangling and my hands in the correct positions, I got the thumbs up and pushed myself out of the plane.

'One thousand, two thousand, three thousand, check canopy.'

This was the initial drill after jumping. It gives a time indication of when the parachute will open after you leave the aircraft.

I looked up and saw the parachute was still in a clump. I looked back down as I was falling to the earth and thought, 'Okay, I have lots of time before I hit the ground so what I'll do is look back up, and if it's still in a clump, I'll release the faulty parachute and fire off the reserve'.

I looked back up and the clump slightly shook in a way that it didn't before. I held my nerve, then relief: it opened. The parachute was in good condition. There were no problems with the lines being twisted or anything so I reached for the handles. Pull left to go left, right to go right, and pull both of them to flare for the landing.

I was loving it. The noisy chaotic rush was over and what was left was a quiet and serene stillness. The initial freefall that was supposed to be 4–6 seconds felt so much longer than it actually was.

I must've counted two or three times as quick because of the adrenaline surge from the jump. I saw some of the others jumping out from the now even smaller-looking plane as I looked up.

As I was hanging in the air, I noticed another parachute person fairly close to me and heading in my direction. The drill for a head-on collision was to pull right.

As he got closer, I felt uneasy that he hadn't noticed me. As we got uncomfortably close to each other, I took evasive action and pulled right. He did the same thing at the exact same time, and we avoided the collision. The seemingly synchronised movement must've looked pretty slick from the ground.

After the near miss incident, I used the handles to pull left and right, enjoying the sights from above whilst plotting my course to the drop zone.

It didn't feel like I was moving at all as I floated down. I did feel movement when I passed through a cloud, though. It felt colder and thicker, and I couldn't see anything. I had always imagined what it would be like to be in a cloud when I was younger, and here I was. It was as close to the flying in my dreams as I'd ever been. I felt free, but I was still attached to a harness and I had no propulsion.

I will always remember a dream from when I was around 7 years old. There was a medieval battle with hundreds of people with swords and shields. I was unarmed and got chased into the top chamber of a castle. I locked the big wooden door behind me and looked around the circular stone-cladded room. There was a small window, like the ones they used to fire arrows out of. The banging on the door got louder and louder. The wood began to splinter, and the door began to give way. I didn't want to be attacked by angry people with swords, so I squeezed through and edged out of the small window space. As the door smashed open, I was halfway out of the window looking down to the ground, which was about 200 feet below. The loud angry soldiers ran towards me with their swords held high. I let myself slide out fully and began to fall to the ground. As I fell, the ground calmly rushed towards me, and at the last second, I swooped upwards and flew with my arms out to the side. Absolute bliss. I doubled back to the window where I jumped from and saw the medieval soldiers looking at me in disbelief. I saw the battle from above and carried on over the rolling hillside. I was effortlessly travelling with speed at will.

I've had many other flying dreams in my life where I could fully control my movements, and others where the control was lessened. It feels easy when it happens, but when my eyes open the easiness fades to impossibility. I'm sure I'll be able to do it one day though with a bit more practice.

The harness I was strapped to had to perform one last trick before I could fully relax.

Remember when I said that pulling both handles would result in a flare? It was close to flare time. We were told in the training that the ground can be deceptive as you approach it. It can look further away or closer depending on the person. The way to overcome this is when you know you're getting close, look down at a 45-degree angle. When you're about 15-20 feet above the ground pull both handles to flare, which will slow you down before you touch down. The flare is designed to rapidly decrease the speed before impact. Flaring too early or too late can be problematic and painful.

As I made the approach to the drop zone, I made sure to be

vigilant about my positioning. I estimated that I was about 20 feet from the ground and pulled both handles. I nailed it. It was a nice smooth landing resulting in my ankles remaining in one piece.

My ecstatic feelings about the experience were soon shaded by the unbelievable pain in my hands as I reeled in the parachute. They were freezing from the coldness above. I didn't really notice it until I reached the ground.

We weren't allowed to wear gloves because they wanted us to be able to operate the handles correctly, or that's what they told us anyway.

As we all came back to earth, we brought our kit over to the truck and shared our glee about what had just happened. What an experience.

For a few weeks after the jump I had this overwhelming feeling of invincibility. I knew I wasn't invincible, but I felt like I was on top of the world and that nothing could hurt me. It was a powerful feeling. I'll never forget passing through the well-endowed proud clouds near Stroud.

Commando Or Don't

I transferred from logistics to the Royal Engineers and joined 59 Independent Commando Squadron. This was a couple years ago before it became 59 Commando Squadron of 24 Commando Engineer Regiment.

A certain amount is known about special forces, marines and paras, but generally people don't know about the five nine army commandos. Under the radar is cool so I won't divulge all the secrets, but I'll give you a taste of what I ate.

The squadron was a small tight knit unit that operated independently from the rest of the Royal Engineers. Within 59 there was Support Troop- in the rear with the gear. Three Troop, otherwise known as Three Tribe- which was my domain. Condor Troop and One Troop were equivalent field troops to the Tribe, and there was the even more discreet and elite, Recce Troop- they operated within the squadron under their own steam and their role was akin to what the Pathfinders got up to.

Transferring from logistics meant that I had to go through lots of training again. I had served for about four years already so I was a step ahead of most in some ways.

People fail commando training all the time from injuries or a lack of will etc. 59 was the path I chose and I made it so. Failure was not an option so there was no lack of will.

Before attaining commando status there was an opportunity to be loaded onto the Army Diver Aptitude course, which I volunteered for. The main driver to be a diver was the pay and the badge. Military divers got hundreds of extra pounds a month for what seemed like a fun job. I always wanted to dive so I put my name down and forgot about it until the first week of the conditioning course.

The conditioning course was what you had to go through before being sent to Lympstone to do the All Arms Commando Course. It was called the 'Beat Up' prior to being called the Conditioning Course and the purpose was to weed out the unworthy and get the worthy up to standard.

That first week of the conditioning course was difficult. They didn't hide the fact that it would be. Our training staff were different to each other but absolute beasts in their own right.

The main guy was an ex- paratrooper who transferred to the PT Corps. He was a firm but fair, dad like leader to us with a good sense of humour. He was a Warrant Officer Class 2, but instead of calling him 'sir', we had to call him 'staff' like his support- two Lance Corporals.

They were good cop and bad cop.

Good cop was an excellent runner who had no fear of heights. He would climb to the top of the 30 foot rope frame and sit on top of it as we climbed. He attacked the bottom field assault course like a greyhound and had a relaxed demeanour. He would often smile and joked around.

Bad cop didn't smile. Bad cop was like the Terminator in looks and in demeanour.

There was a ring of dust in the summer and mud in the winter. We would have to crawl around that ring which was located on the bottom field assault course. We joked that bad cop was not born, but forged, and appeared in the ring like

Arnie in the film. Not only was he built like a body builder, he was a quick runner and I never saw him slow down on a run.

These three elite level soldiers made our lives hell at points, but taught us well and moulded us into the shape of commandos.

Those who volunteered for the diver aptitude had the choice of going to Whale Island in Portsmouth to do the course, or drop out and stay to complete week two of the conditioning course. I heard rumours about the aptitude but, week three and beyond was looming and I stuck to the plan. The diving aptitude was Monday to Friday, with Friday being a half day. Naively, I thought it would be easier than the hardships of the conditioning course regardless of the rumours. It wasn't. It was one of the hardest things I've ever done.

Over the previous years before my time, the training staff had built a culture of breaking people, which eventually got phased out after my time. It changed because the arduousness was gratuitous and too many blokes were getting injured.

The navy divers did their course in the same place, but had a vastly different experience. They concentrated on the diving, whereas we concentrated on heart rate. They justified the savage treatment by saying that we would be able to stay under water for longer if we were fitter. If our cardio was improved, we would use less air and we'd be more effective.

The first thing we did on day one was line up to sign for the equipment that we'd be using for the week. This was normal, nothing out of the ordinary. Next was the camp acquaintance.

This was an orientation- getting to know where things are on the camp and how things work etc, but with a twist. We had to run with all of the stuff that we had just signed for above our heads.

It was probably only a couple miles or more, or less. I don't know. All I know is that it was savage. This was just a taste of what was to come. Running with all that stuff above your head for all that time seemed impossible. I had to rest the weight on the top of my head when the D.S weren't looking. Everyone did. The orientation turned to disorientation. Press ups, leopard crawls, squats, squat thrusts, sit ups, sprints, monkey runs etc. We hadn't even got changed yet. I had rips on my trousers and cuts on my arms from a camp acquaintance.

Things went from bad to worse when I ran past a poor bloke who was screaming in agony on the floor through an injury. This was a sign of things to come. The D.S made sure that we left the injured in place for them to deal with because it was an individual effort. Welcome to the Diver Aptitude!

I assume he got sent back to his unit after a trip to the medical centre, as did many others. R.T.U (return to unit) was not on my agenda.

The course started with 35-40 people, many of which were para, commando and PT trained. I was an un-badged craphat in the eyes of some but that wasn't going to phase me.

The official daily PT sessions would last for three or more hours at a time and we had a couple of those a day. Half way through the sessions the staff would change hands, adding a new energy to which we had to keep up with.

We were constantly being pushed. Even commando trained 59 lads failed the course. This helped to push me forward- if I could get through this then I could pass the Conditioning and All Arms courses.

We worked 20 hour days wearing the same clothes throughout. The few times of actually being under the water was like a holiday. A break from the hell above. It was a bit like in Men of Honour where they had to put together pipes and stuff using tools under the water. This part was actually quite enjoyable.

To convey to you the difficulty of the course, I'll tell you about when we were on a PT session in dry suits (which we would have to get in and out of many, many times following the command; 'AWKWARD!').

On this particular PT session, we came to a platform with various levels. It was overlooking the lake and was easily the height of a house, probably much higher. We were made to climb to the top and jump off into the water below whilst in our dry suits and wearing our fins. It was to test our mettle and make sure we carried out the drill correctly.

You would have to point your toes downwards so the fins enter the water in the most hydrodynamic way. This ensures that you avoid injury.

I got to the top and I did not care about the height hhhhwhatsoever. I stepped off and breathed in a sigh of relief as I plummeted down. I was weightless for a few seconds and it felt incredible. A micro moment in time where my body totally relaxed as I fell from the precarious height.

It was a much appreciated rest that quickly ended as I rose up out of the water with my fist above my head shouting, 'Diver well!', as I surfaced from the cold lake.

The course was horrible. People who seemed fitter than me quit. People got injured and left but I was one of the nine that passed and was eligible to be loaded onto a future diver course. It was a proud moment.

There was a two or three year window to do the course in, but I decided to let it go in the end.

It wasn't something I really wanted to do. The money would have been nice, but I wasn't very inspired about being in the dive store away from the Tribe. I took the opportunity of completing an arduous course within an arduous course and I looked forward to what was next.

I was apprehensive about week three of the conditioning course.

To my relief, myself and another lad, Dave who passed the aptitude with me were given light duties as a reward for passing. Week three was relatively chilled out for us. It was very well received, and very much required.

As commandos in training, we would do hundreds and hundreds of pull ups and press ups during the week. Rope climbing, running and yomping were also bread and butter activities.

If you don't know what yomping is, check it out online or the next line.

Yomping; To walk quickly interspersed with sporadic running whilst carrying heavy equipment over any terrain- usually difficult terrain.

One of the bottom field tests at Lympstone was a 30 foot rope climb carrying 21lbs of weight, plus a rifle. The assault course at Chivenor (where 59 were based) was designed to mimic the one at Lympstone, but was made to be harder than their official set up. For example, the ropes at Chiv were thicker than the ones at Lympstone. This meant that more grip strength was required to reach the top of the rope.

About three quarters of the way through the Conditioning Course, there were several of us with the same painful symptoms that effected us all slightly differently.

After a bottom field session, which is tantamount to torture, I went back to the accommodation and laid down on the floor of my room for about an hour in absolute agony.

It was tendonitis of the elbow. This type of tendonitis was contracted through sustained arduous activity in the form of pulling. I had tears in my eyes from the volatile intense constant deep throbbing dull and sharp pain that would not dissipate. As I laid in agony, I imagined if this would hinder my chances of being loaded onto the course at Lympstone.

My mind could get me through but could my body? Our ex-para leader had seen it all before.

His goal was to prepare us for what the Royal Marine instructors had in store for us.

He needed to see that as well as being fully prepared in terms of kit, knowledge, drills and mindset, we needed to confidently be able to climb the rope with weight, complete a regain on a horizontal rope with weight, and of course be able to do all the running and pull ups etc.

I was allowed to continue on with the conditioning course whilst avoiding pulling exercises. This would give me the time to heal enough before going down to Lympstone.

As long as I could demonstrate that I could complete the mandatory tasks at the end of the Conditioning Course, I was good to go.

The final week of the conditioning course was a lot more relaxed. They didn't want to risk any unnecessary injuries so close to the start of the All Arms Commando Course.

That being said, we went on the traditional obligatory mud run on the week before heading to Lympstone. This was a rite of passage with a group photo taken at the end with everyone covered head to toe in dark sludge.

The wet, smelly, silty ground was difficult to move through, but great fun at the same time.

We got to a steep bank where bad cop shouted, 'Come on lads!', and threw himself down it sliding on his belly. We all followed him and dove down the slippery surface face forward like you would on a water park slide.

As I made contact with the soft shiny surface I recoiled and my thoughts raced.

I smashed my right knee on a camouflaged rock. I stayed still for while and when the initial shock of the pain lessened, I limped on. I was hoping that it would pass, but I knew it wouldn't.

We were a few miles from camp and I had to keep going to get back.

I eventually made the D.S aware of my situation and they gave me the opportunity to be driven back to camp. I refused their offer and made it back under my own steam.

Following this annoying set back, I was exempt from all

physical training until being tested to see if I was ready for Lympstone a few days later.

I got through it all with no real problems. I had constant pain (for years later), but it was manageable. I was faced with the All Arms Commando Course with an injured knee and a painful elbow. I rested as much as I could and avoided anything that could exacerbate the injuries.

After jumping through all the hoops and proving myself, I was there. Carrying a couple of injuries here and there but ready for the challenge.

The All Arms Commando course was made up of a mixture of volunteers from every part of the British military. The occasional foreign military personnel would also attempt it, which I only found out about on the course. We had a really tall Dutch officer with us who made it to the end.

There were over a hundred volunteers, with engineers taking the biggest proportion, then artillery, then logistics, then others like infantry, RAF, and I can't remember who else.

The 59 Engineers stood out as the most prepared. Our kit and admin was of a much higher standard than the others. The artillery were not too far off our heels, but regardless of our differences, we were all on the same team and worked together.

The first week was very easy in comparison to our previous training. I knew this would be the case so I made the most of it because I knew the tempo would increase as the course went on.

The All Arms Commando Course lasted for 13 weeks, most of which was spent out on exercise with assault course training and theory lessons taking place in between.

It's a bit of a blur to me now. I took each day as it came and had my sights on completion.

I remember the wet and dry drills. It was something that a lot of people didn't like, but I did see the benefit and eventually enjoyed it.

The idea is to take your wet and muddy combat uniform off, place it under your sleeping bag, (which was inside the outer waterproof bivi bag liner protecting the sleeping bag). You then change into some clean and dry combats as you slept in your sleeping bag.

The unpleasant part that people hated was when you had to get up. You changed back into the horrible wet combats and stowed the clean combats away. The idea is to keep your sleeping bag clean and dry so that you have a nice environment to sleep in. The reason people don't like doing it is because when it's minus 2 degrees with snow on the ground and you have to get out of your warm sleeping bag at 2am to go on sentry in wet combats, it doesn't feel that great.

Commando training is well documented with the Royal Marines Commandos, but the All Arms Commando Course is not as well known to people. The main difference is that the marines start off as civilians and work their way through, whereas the All Arms is made up of trained soldiers. The treatment is slightly different. As trained soldiers we were pushed harder and expected to do more. There was less sympathy because we were expected to be of a higher calibre- pre commando training courses etc.

There was a rivalry between Royal Marines and the commando trained army 'Pongo's'. Everyone thought they were the best. However, I did overhear Royal Marine instructors agreeing that the All Arms was more difficult than the Royal Marines' training.

An example of this being the case was on the final exercise of my all arms commando course.

It took place on Dartmoor and the weather was the worst it had been for 20 years. A severe storm had hit the Devonshire training area, and on these particular couple of days and nights there were 80mph winds. Grape sized hail stones flew horizontally onto us. We had to tip our heads to the right as we yomped so the hail hit our helmets instead of our faces. Civilians were being evacuated off the area, and to make my point, the Royal Marine recruit troops were taken off the moors for safety reasons. The All Arms continued forward.

It took us all night to get to our final check point where the D.S were waiting for us. We were way over schedule but we all made it. They saw our condition and we were rewarded with a few extra hours sleep with no sentry duty. We needed it.

It's difficult to put across how hard these feats of endurance and perseverance are. Imagine carrying 70-80 kilos or more for hours and hours, up and down steep bumpy uneven terrain, with horizontal hail smashing into you in almost pitch black winter conditions on top of weeks and weeks of previous physical and mental punishment. I had to do it twice.

One of the D.S had a bit of fun and made us wrestle each other on our knees in the woods on the last day of the final exercise. I cut my knee, which immediately got infected with the notorious Woodbury rash. The pain got to the point where I had to say something to the D.S.

After an inspection they sent me to the medical centre. My knee area was swollen, red and very painful. They drew around the redness to see if it was tracking further up my body. After a couple of hours the pain increased and the redness had spread. I was laid up in bed in the medical centre building for a week having to take over 30 pills per day.

I was told that because of the high spread rate of the infection, I would've been dead in a couple of days if I had no medical intervention. The pain was excruciating and I was off the course. R.T.U.

All I had to do was the final week, which was the commando tests. One test per day and that was it. I was devastated.

I eventually got sent back to Chiv. I hoped that I could get loaded onto the next course to do the test week only, but this was not my fate.

The squadron went to the arctic to do winter warfare training in Norway.

My course mates were off to Scandinavia wearing green berets with daggers on their arms and I was left behind.

I eventually got my second chance. I had to do the final exercise again and test week. The second final exercise was tough, but not as bad as the first one. I knew what to expect this time and the weather wasn't as bad. I bantered with the lads about doing a final ex when it was a final ex.

This bravado soon came back to bite me.

Test week effected people differently. Some found it easy and others like myself found it very challenging. The 9 miler was the easiest test for me. The endurance course was hard because you don't know how you're doing for time. If you run in over the time you fail.

I did it as fast as I could and fired the shots hitting the required amount of targets and passed. On the run back before the shots, about a mile from the camp, there was an older gentleman walking his dog. He said to me; 'keep going, it's only pain'. These simple words of encouragement meant so much to me. It was like my dad was there pushing me forward. He always said, 'it's only pain', whenever I hurt myself growing up.

I knew that he ran along this same path years before to earn his green beret. It was a poignant moment for me and it helped me to pass that test.

I'd only been on the Tarzan course twice before. Once on the previous All Arms and once on this course. At the time, I would say it was my least favourite test. The initial high wire stuff was quite fun but technical. I had to really pay attention to what the others were doing and copy them to get through it.

Going back to the differences between the All Arms and Royal Marine training. They had many more tutorials and attempts before actually being tested. I personally had even less training than what the All Arms got. It was a proper a lung bleeder- 13 minutes to complete the high wire stuff, the bottom field assault course then back up to the 30 foot wall. Like the endurance test, it's an individual timed event. You had to go as hard and fast as you could. When I reached the top of the 30 foot wall at the end, I felt such relief that I would never have to do it again.

One more to go. Tarzan was hard, but the worst was yet to

come. The final event- the 30 miler. All that stood in the way of me becoming a commando was a 30 mile jaunt across the unforgiving Dartmoor terrain in under 8 hours and carrying about 20 kilos of weight.

It was made up of five, six mile legs with a minute or two break between each one. We were given bananas and a pasty along the route for energy, as well as hot goffers- which is warm juice and a funny naval slang word.

It was a staggered event with a D.S leading a section of hopefuls at different times. I think there was six groups from what I remember. I was in the second group. The first leg of six was fine. I felt comfortable and optimistic. There was one weak link in the chain who was nursing an injury. He was slowing us down and would've made the whole section fail if we stayed at his pace. The D.S made this clear to him and he stopped at the first leg, failing the course.

I don't know what happened from then on, but I was absolutely drained. I became the weak link in the section.

One of the 59 lads in my section joked about me months later saying that he'd never seen someone run 24miles with his eyes shut before.

I had to keep running ahead of the squad on the flats and downhills and they would catch me on the up hills. I dug as deep as I could to get through it. The 29 Artillery D.S corporal leading our section, who later went into the special forces, kept threatening to leave me behind. I was constantly running ahead after falling behind and pushing and pushing with the image in my mind of how it would be if I failed. He kept telling me to stop, but I didn't. I couldn't leave without my green beret.

As we approached the bridge signalling the end of the march, he told us to fix up and look presentable in an orderly squad. I crossed that finish line with my head held high.

The emotions of it all soon hit me and others alike. Everything that I'd done in my career had led up to this moment. I was now part of the commando brotherhood.

The Artillery D.S gave me some words of encouragement. He said that I 'displayed true commando spirit', and shook my hand. I sat down on my own away from everyone for a minute and wiped the tears from my eyes. I gathered myself and shook the hands of my colleagues and friends.

I got handed my coveted green beret and looked forward to what was next. I learned that I'd be joining Three Tribe and the next chapter began.

Forever In Det

Commando training was very tough as you can imagine, but the Royal Engineers' Combat Engineering course was pretty tough too. It was about three months long and we had two Five Nine D.S on my course, which added to the work rate as you can also imagine.

The course consisted of bridging, water supply, general field engineering, watermanship, mine warfare and I, like many others, enjoyed the explosive demolitions part of the combat engineering course.

Our practical introduction to the subject came with a demonstration of the dangers.

Some people assume that it's only the plastic explosive- PE4 (C4 for the Americans) that's the only dangerous component. The detonator and detonating cord needs just as much respect, and in fact, probably more respect. The detonator is the metallic cigarette shaped part that gets plunged into the pliable PE4 explosive. The det cord is attached to the det and safety fuse is attached to the det cord- this is the basic set up.

The detonator doesn't look like much, but it's volatile. Prior to our practical lesson we were shown a picture of a US Marine who tried to crimp a det to some det cord using his teeth. Let's just say that we handled those dets like they were ready to blow at any second.

The practical lesson was designed to give us some hands on experience with how to use the equipment, as well as cementing respect for the dangers.

We used the safety fuse attached to the det cord, attached to a det, which was then placed inside a pigs head- local farms donated bodiless pigs for these demonstrations.

We carried out the drills and lit the fuse. I have no idea why that American put that det anywhere near his face, and I remember thinking that I'd never make the same mistake of being injured by demolition equipment, or so I hoped.

A couple years ago whilst doing some demolition training with 59 at a range, I got hit by shrapnel from an exploding detonator.

It was a particularly hot summery day and we were digging in wooden targets to blow up using different types of explosives and methods. The muddy ground was bone dry and very difficult to excavate. We were using pick axes and shovels to get the job done, which made it even more arduous. Mechanical assistance would've been nice but we didn't have that luxury.

We had already dug two sets of eight targets in and blown them up to see the effects and differences. We were on our final dig in and detonation before knocking off for the day. As I swung the pick axe above my head to drive it into the ground, there was a loud bang and instant pain to my side.

We weren't in a war zone but my training took over. I zigzagged to proven ground keeping low and away from the blast whilst being mindful of a potential secondary hit. I moved about 20 metres away and looked around at all the confusion and pain. There were six or seven of us who sustained minor injuries and I still have a scar near my ribs from the incident to this day.

There were small cuts, bruises and trickles of blood amongst the handful of us. There worst injury was a cut on the face about an inch below the eye. He was lucky he didn't lose his sight.

There were no life threatening injuries, but there was some serious dit spinning (story telling) afterwards.

After the blast we all moved to a safe area and cleaned ourselves up. We waited for the investigation to be completed. A couple hours passed and the Ammunition Technicians concluded that the impact of the pick axe had struck the tip of an old detonator that had already been used. It got chalked up to being a freak accident but the protocol was updated. A minimum of a t-shirt must be worn on top whilst working on the range, regardless of the weather.

After I was chosen for G.S.C training there was a certain amount of information that was divulged to me. Their network was extensive and solid, and emphasis was placed on finding the right people for the work. Recruitment consisted of tests that were often unbeknownst to the subject.

The 'old det from a previous group' was a clever way to test people's reactions on home soil and in a relatively safe environment- who overreacted, who under reacted, who remained calm and vigilant, who looked for direction and who took charge. This was one isolated test based on a lifetime of observation. All members of G.S.C units were vetted from childhood and monitored onwards.

One Flew Over The Afghan Mess

We had a troop holiday to Kavos before our Op Herrick 9 tour.

We wanted to have a blow out before the potential of being blown up.

I drank so much Sambuca that I vomited blood on the last day. The lining between my mouth and stomach had given way and nothing other than blood came up. It rivals Dermorhea and I don't recommend it.

After delays, the day finally came and I flew into Kandahar on an RAF Tristar plane- an old white civilian looking plane that turned it's lights off before landing to avoid rocket attacks. We actually had to circle the area before landing because of an attack on the base. My first bit of excitement. After a short stay in K.A.F, I moved to Camp Bastion before being helo'd out to the FOB.

The not so yellow Sea King Helicopter dropped off men and post at a couple more FOB's (Inkerman and Kajaki) before I landed at my final destination of Forward Operating Base Sangin in the Helmand Province of Afghanistan. This area was my home for the next four months.

After I got settled in and got the lay of the land, I acted.

I single handedly built the infrastructure necessary for the local Afghans to thrive. I rebuilt a school in a day.

I supplied clean water to thousands within a week.

I defeated the Taliban in the area by force, but mainly by changing their minds. I made them chill out with all the fear and death stuff- they became nice and friendly. One of them married the Commanding Officers daughter and a peace deal was agreed.

Peace was everywhere. Around every corner peace reigned supreme. The air stunk of peace. You couldn't escape the stench of harmony and nor did we want to.

This wasn't well received by some politicians and war makers, so they swept it under the rug and I was sent home under the cover of darkness and under the pretence of 'administrative leave'.

All records of my victories and achievements were scrubbed from the record and hidden.

Anyone who knew of me and my achievements were coerced, blackmailed and advised to keep quiet. Their plan was in motion and I was a spanner in their works. The war had to go on for a few more years to attain the correct finances, artefacts, ground, people, knowledge and intelligence before victory could be officially declared.

In hindsight they wanted the Taliban to take control under their lead, and I was a problem.

The day before I was extracted from Tangiers to Sangin, the unmistakable sound of a bullet flew directly over my head about 30 feet above the ground.

I looked in the direction of where it came from, but it was clear.

The ground features dictated that we weren't being directly attacked, so I carried on doing what I was doing but with heightened awareness.

Another bullet whizzed past, but lower than the first one.

One more came in and smashed into a post a few feet from me and about six foot above my head. I took appropriate cover and waited until it was deemed clear.

As I suspected it turned out to be nothing. Just overspill from a firefight happening a small distance away, or so I was told.

This was my last taste of action in Afghan before I was forced into a different situation. I wondered if I really did dodge the bullet.

They gave me an offer that I couldn't refuse and made me sign a stronger form of N.D.A.

I cant say too much, but let's just say that my time following commando life was, out of this world. I won't go into detail about being a Galactic Space Commando who went on liaison missions to far away planets and moons, because it would be in violation of the secrecy pact.

Certain TV shows and films are pretty spot on, so I suggest watching them for more information. Stargate SG1 and Star Trek The Next Generation sprinkled with some Full Metal Jacket pretty much sums it up.

I didn't break the non disclosure agreement by saying this by the way, because this is fiction remember.

If I do end up getting 'suicided', it wasn't suicide. Prove I died by what they said. Peruse their files that shows I'm dead. Confused by lies that's in their head, I refuse to die by man instead, I won't die. Plus, the female offspring of the Royal Flagel Deckerons at Site 012481 dipped me in the Penclouditus Brankipinge, so I'm certain I can't die before my time anyway.

Maybe the difference in atmospheric conditions will have an

effect, but those Flagel Deckerons seemed pretty adamant that I'd be protected. Time will tell.

As I said, I can't go into detail, but when you bring together two warring nations from a moon that's half the size of ours who've been fighting for generations, you tend to get rewarded even if you resist it. You're simply doing your job at the end of the day, and doing what's right is how it should be. Not receiving gratitude from someone who really wants to give it to you can sometimes appear to be disrespectful, so I obliged.

It had a 100% success record for millions of species and peoples, so I accepted. The Penclouditus Brankipinge has different effects on different peoples. The R.F.D's catalogued the effect on different beings. For us humans it provides a kind of dimensional/spiritual protection that sees you to your deathday date uninterrupted.

It doesn't mean that I can jump off buildings and expect to be okay- it means that outside forces can't encroach on my timeline.

Cregulifong- the daughter of the R.F.D king (who I called Fong. I tried Creg but it sounded too much like Craig and it seemed inappropriate considering our close relationship) assured me that my immune system, brain function and biomechanics would also be given a kind of boost from the Penclouditus Brankipinge. Not in a drug or body modification way, more of a celluelectro auroric force amplification that's without risk of harm. So far I feel great.

I can't divulge any further in terms of back story, but the opposition to the R.F.D's, called the Hwati, claim the R.F.D's encroached uninvited with intentions other to which the Hwati wished to indulge. The action caused harm, but the R.F.D's people survival depended on it.

A pure and binding agreement amongst all participants can happen, but the feeling of closure can fade over time. It can resurface at a later date under a new perception of the details.

If you bury the hatchet too shallow, it will be dug up. Throw it in the fire. Let the wood burn and cast the blade in a new shape and celebrate in a ritualistic manner. That's what I always say.

DMT Or Coffee?

The military I was immersed in was an anti- drugs organisation, apart from the use of alcohol, tobacco and caffeine- let's ignore the Pen Brank. Even though I was indoctrinated to be anti drugs, I knew there were different levels to it. Some drugs are worse than others- heroin compared to cannabis for example.

When I was in the process of leaving the forces, I knew that I wanted to experience psychedelics as a civilian. I was interested in experimenting with magic mushrooms, LSD and maybe weed. I didn't know about DMT at that time. I felt like hallucinating was conducive with mental endurance and the enhanced visual beauty of nature. It interested and intrigued me enough to want to experience it.

My mental endurance level compared to the average human is relatively high, so I knew that I wouldn't panic under the influence and jump out of a window. I did actually experience hallucinations whilst in the military, but without the use of any substances. Sleep deprivation can cause visual hallucinations. A lack of sleep is difficult to understand if you haven't had to deal with it. Doing an all nighter, or getting 4hrs sleep a day because of a newborn, or working through the night is one thing. When you're physically pushed to your limits whilst being mentally on high alert for days at a time, sleeping outside in the dead of winter and eating ration pack food, it's quite a different thing in comparison.

Shivering in a sleeping bag whilst trying to sleep for two hours before being woken up to go on sentry duty was not a situation in which I could relax and drift off into the unconscious. Many others could, but for me, sleeping out in the field was almost impossible.

There was an occasion where my body needed to replenish so much that I slept for a couple minutes, stood up, leaning against a tree. When I snapped back to life, I was shocked that I was able to sleep whilst stood up. I knew it wasn't a micro sleep because I was with someone who walked off and came back a minute or two later; his footsteps were the reason I woke up.

The first time I hallucinated was on a march during a reconnaissance detail. Myself and two others had to accompany a Captain on a mission to observe, and possibly disrupt enemy positions.

It was quite a cold night so I was wearing an issued green fleece over my t-shirt and under my combat jacket. It was three nights into the week long exercise, so my tiredness levels were quite high at this point. This was years before becoming a commando, so my levels of robustness were still being cultivated.

As we set off, I quickly warmed up because of the fleece.

Up hills, down hills, through bushes and trees. No thrills, back kills, a few rushes of breeze.

The night grew older, minutes to hours. Eyes wide shut, dreaming of cold showers. There she is, rocking on the right. Indifferent glances, try to be polite.

As I was marching along wondering when it would end, I saw an old lady on a rocking chair two feet off the path to my right hand side. I was so exhausted that I didn't really acknowledge what had happened. I remember thinking with total indifference,

'Oh look, there's an old woman on a rocking chair'. It was so clear and real that it seemed normal, but it wasn't normal. Why would there be an old woman in a military training area in the middle of the night rocking on a chair and acknowledging me?

I concluded after the patrol was over that I hallucinated. Then again, it could have been a ghost! The reconnaissance, or recce (pronounced rekky) was quite uneventful. We saw an enemy position with too much man power for us to deal with, so we made some notes and came back to the harbour area.

(A harbour area is where you set up a secure camp location whilst on exercise.

The perimeter of the harbour area is guarded by continuously manned sentry positions which cover all angles for total all round protection. The size and shape of the harbour area, as well as the features of the ground, determines where and how many sentry positions there are).

On the commando course, I had an impressive visual hallucination that trumps most induced by chemical compounds.

There was a section of us detailed for a standing patrol. It was on the Woodbury Common training area near Lympstone about half way through the course. A standing patrol is where you yomp/march to a designated place on the map, set up a basic harbour area and wait for the enemy to show up. The aim is to keep still and quiet and observe for enemy patrols. If they appear, you either engage with them or stealthily gather intelligence, depending on the mission.

Our orders were to stay until the enemy showed up. If they didn't appear, we would head back to the main harbour area at the agreed upon time. I can't remember if we were supposed to engage with or gather intelligence, but it doesn't matter- it was cold and boring. Nothing happened for hours and hours. People were dropping off to sleep as time went on. I couldn't.

A character trait that my body adopted was being extremely tired as soon as the sun went down- with my mind keeping it awake, then when the sun came back up again, I was wide awake, regardless of how little sleep I had.

There would often be small windows of opportunity during daylight hours for sleep, but because the sun was up, I found it so difficult to sleep properly.

I once counted how many hours sleep I had in a five day period on the commando course. It was 8. It got to the point where every member of the standing patrol was asleep apart from me.

I generally don't like to wake people up, and because I was up, it felt like I was looking after them while they rested. I stared into the direction of where the enemy patrol would approach from with eagerness. There was a small shrub in front of me that caught my attention.

This was the moment of the vivid visuals. The shrub was a reverse silhouette to the black of the night. What happened next can only be described as a cartoon light show of astonishing proportions. This inanimate bush surged into colourful light as it transformed from one object to the next with clockwork precision.

I laid in wonder as the image of a car turned into a cowboy, to a table, to a bicycle, and on and on to vastly different creations within the same shape of the shrub. What was even more insane, other than the colours and details, was the fact that the image would change at one second intervals.

A conveyor belt of magic that no one else could see was being shown to me. I was beaming with delight and nodded my head along to the beat of the image change.

I looked away at the men to my left and right then looked back to see if it would carry on displaying images, and it did.

After a while it did fade away and eventually the activity ceased. I laid there reliving the strange and beautiful occurrence in my mind until my attention was brought to some movement in the distance to my front. We were a tactical patrol so I didn't want to make the wrong decision by overreacting to a fox or a mouse or something. Sound in a dark forest travels far. A small creatures movements can make it seem much larger than it actually is.

I bided my time until I was sure. It was too loud and big sounding to be a small creature so I clicked my safety catch off. The sound echoed around the trees, then I followed up with the command, 'Halt!'.

There was some stirring amongst the sleeping soldiers as they perked up to the potential intruder. The movement ahead paused for a few seconds, and then carried on as if ignoring my request.

I repeated the instruction then all hell broke loose.

It was one of the D.S (Directing Staff/instructors) who opened fire first.

I immediately returned fire as did the men to my left and

right. The others not in the line of sight fell back, then myself and the other shooters moved back firing and moving, as is the way.

The D.S called it off and sent us back to the main harbour area for sleep and sentry duty until the morning.

It reminded me of the woman in the rocking chair from years earlier, but this was on a different level. The detail, colour and precision made me question whether or not it came from my mind or somewhere else. The old lady on the rocking chair was strange, but it seemed like a hallucination. This time it seemed like there was a lot more substance and intelligence to it.

Maybe it was because I was a few years older and my brain was more developed compared to before. Or it was another ghost. Either way, I'm glad they both happened, and I'm even more glad that the D.S didn't find us all sleeping!

DMT is quite well known about these days, even though it's still very much a mystery. The experience is difficult to recreate with words, and maybe it shouldn't be. Maybe it should be seen and felt by the right people rather than being written about and discussed. Either way I won't be subjecting you to my thoughts and experiences with it because it won't do it the justice it deserves. I do however want to explain what happened when I came across 25 grams of San Pedro cactus powder, also known as mescaline.

I was offered it by a free spirited, bare footed young man who I sometimes trained with a couple years ago. The training was a weekly, two hour, free-for-all at a gymnastics gym. There were foam pits to jump into, ropes to climb, a bouncy floor, box jumps, trampolines, climbing walls and various other equipment to play with.

I'd like to take this opportunity to say that I'm not advocating the use of substances, especially if you're not mentally prepared and ready for their feedback. If you do decide to experiment with them; where you are, who you are with, and what your state of mind is, are the three key factors that should be considered prior to dosing yourself. I've used hallucinogens for inner endurance training and to give me a more rounded view on humans and the nature of reality and insight.

San Pedro cactus powder was a new one for me at the time, linked closer to shamanism. I heard stories of transformative feelings and visions, communications with unknown entities who appear knowledgable of ones life, and who can provide insight into the universe.

I needed to see it for myself. I planned it for a Saturday because I was off work for the weekend. With no work the next day, my mind was clear and I prepared myself. I packed a backpack with extra clothes, some food, two litres of water and my pocket stuff like wallet, keys and my turned off phone. All was contained in waterproof inner bags in the backpack, commando style.

The mission was to infiltrate the forest and patrol unknown ground without being detected, whilst mashed on mescaline.

At around 10am and with an empty stomach, I poured the 25grams of the lime green powder into a pint glass and topped it up with water. After stirring the bitty mixture, I took my first sip.

Absolutely disgusting!

After 30 minutes of holding my nose and breathing through my mouth, gagging with diaphragm contractions, I finally sunk the entirety with water in my eyes and a bubbly stomach.

I chewed gum on the way to the bus stop to disguise the foul taste.

The 25 minute ride to the woods passed by rather quickly. I distracted myself with other thoughts and listened to my iPod.

My aim was to go to a part of the woods where other people would not be.

There was a small stream running parallel to the path with a fallen tree creating a bridge to the other side. The other side was a steep wooded climb to an unknown peak. I had never seen anyone traverse this severe slope, and my instincts told me it was the place to be. Once the coast was clear, I darted across and ran up the hill without being seen. I felt a sense of relief as I transcended above the man-made track up to the untouched forest habitat above. The higher I climbed, the further away the human sounds became.

For the next hour or so, I quietly explored the area with the sickly pain in my stomach testing my patience. I withheld from vomiting as I thought it would lessen the effects, and therefore the experience. I distracted myself with the beauty of what was around me.

I saw remnants of old farming equipment, rusting and decaying into the earth. I saw unused paths that had been taken over by plant life. The trees were full and lush and I was surrounded by the sounds of birds. I was in an area that hadn't been touched by humans for many years. It was my own personal temporary domain up high away from the disruption of human traffic.

The focus from the sickly feeling shifted to a shaky physical vibration that affected my body and vision. My eyeballs felt heavier and I lacked full control over them. It was controllable, but the effects manifested and were overwhelming compared to normal consciousness. After I became accustomed to the new sensations, I saw the forest in a bright new light. The sickness was replaced with an absolute connection to the natural world around me.

For over two hours I edged through the undergrowth, pausing after almost every step to drink in the sights and sounds. I navigated silently through overgrown bushes and precarious ground barefoot like an apex predator. I would stare intently at otherwise unimportant objects like sticks and leaves for minutes at a time, studying their energy and form. The details flooded into my eyes with a depth of almost mutual understanding.

The light rain that wetted the forest barely touched my clothes as I moved strategically with utter feeling and knowing. My mind was clear and focussed throughout on the actions of my movement, and on my life in general.

My mind would wonder off and reflect on things, like past conflicts and the people in my life. My cognition was sound enough, and I made informed decisions about what I was doing.

There was a small steam train line that ran almost parallel to the path and the stream below.

A steam engine rolled along the line releasing plumes of

clouds which bellowed out the front of the huge iron horse. The noise from the horn reverberated through the natural peace of my realm.

I could not ignore it. I moved to the perfect location to see what was going on and looked on in amazement. I felt like the indigenous people at the end of the film Apocalypto- watching the alien looking wooden Spanish ships near the shore.

I knew at the time that it was only an old train, but the feeling I got from it was like I was seeing it for the first time.

Once it left the area, I reflected on all of this and on how much I was enjoying myself. The initial sickness wasn't very fun, but everything else was incredible.

I moved to a less dense part of the forest, near to where the dead farming equipment was. The sickness finally passed.

The trees were tall and green and everything felt actively alive. I stared upwards towards the canopy in the direction of twenty or thirty birds chattering. My focus onto them meant that my body stayed statue still. After a short period of time, I noticed the small birds bouncing around the branches and becoming closer to my position. The sparrow like creatures seemed to notice me, and were curious. Their quick movements and body language displayed intelligent interest as they observed me.

One after another, they relayed from branch to branch until they were no more than 15 feet away. The connection I felt from the plant life was now visible in the animal life.

The potential pivotal moment of physical contact between myself and my feathered friends was rudely interrupted by a small crashing noise behind me.

My body remained still as my focus switched to what it could be.

I was 90% sure that it was just a branch falling to the forest floor from a tree, but I wasn't 100% sure. What if I had been compromised by an unwanted observer?

I had to make a decision to either ignore it, or quickly turn around to confirm what it was.

My eyes never left the birds during this decision process, and I could see that they had settled where they were and weren't approaching any further.

I gently turned at my waist to check the area behind, and after two or three seconds I turned back around to find empty branches. The birds' curiosity had extinguished and they moved on.

I really appreciated the interaction and reflected on what the falling of the branch meant. Distractions from what's important at the present moment can force the loss, or force the process of losing what you really want. Focus is important. Wherever your focus lays is how your life plays.

59 Bullets And Beer On The Wall

I've seen enough.

I used to be out in woods with tanks and tents firing guns and stuff, out in thunder rough, hungry running buff, taking cover 'nuff, pull up push up digging ditch blowing charge we tough, here we come you lot marching to your spot, laden weighing 40 stocks praying day not hunting fox, many X-Ray Rentgen shots, plural dental healthcare slots, probably get replaced by bots got properly wet from all the sets no stopping shopping discount vets.

I've seen enough.

Twenty rucks plenty trucks paid for things in baat and bucks, cradled human life and such, been all over fed the ducks, eaten bugs fish eyes and crocs, Spanish salad chicken pox, spraying aiming 40 shots. How many know their deathday date? Birthday birthday death day date, and how many shots get wasted brain dead aim head bullet trap catch that safety off then on, move in closer to them come from the side but enemy's gone.

Armoured whips and drones Apache battle ships ringing off satellite phones, I lay in dust with 'nades, rifle cocked and ready I'm one in the whole brigade, old heads looking at us, yompin' through their space seeing their culture fade, people die all the time in horrible ways get paid in blades but some of em can be saved we all behave in a way true say environment affects our day to day.

PART TWO – FORCE

Alive Or Twist

A couple years ago before I became a commando, the plane I was on got redirected to Bolton Airport on the way to Boston from Berlin. The routine BA flight got battered with birds and we had to land urgently. It was an uneventful and controlled descent and landing, to the delight of all on board.

As we were rolling to the planes parking place, a brazen voice bellowed out from the first class section. I was located just behind so I managed to catch the brash back and forth between him and the seasoned flight attendant.

'Hey stewardess! I have somewhere to be, how long is this gonna take?'.

In a polite and informative manner she said something to the effect of; how long is a piece of string? I don't know what his exact response was but he seemed to find what she said funny.

We awaited our fate onboard- fix the issue, or transfer to a different aircraft. The inpatient passenger carried on making a fuss- demanding answers and ordering staff to bring drinks etc. Although he was a bit annoying for everyone around him, I found it entertaining watching all the humans react to his actions. I especially found him entertaining because of his bold manner and big ego. His appearance was an amalgamation of various characters that I'd seen before- A gruff look similar to Tommy Lee Jones, but with a more youthful energy and features akin to Matthew McConaughey when he was a younger man. The expensive looking cowboy boots and blue jeans he was wearing gave him that Texas look, and I wish he had the cowboy hat to match.

After about an hour, news came to us through the speaker system from the pilot. There were 237 passengers on board and planes were being diverted to pick us up in groups.

The cowboy had been on his phone to various people throughout the hour and had a call back right after the pilots announcement. I didn't hear his conversations, but I did hear his abrupt announcement.

'I've got one space on a private jet, who's in?'.

As quick as a gun flash I shouted, 'Yes!' and stood up.

He looked at me in a way that made me think he was making the offer to one of the female passengers, but he reconciled, nodded, then said, 'Alright, let's go gringo!'.

I only had hand luggage with me so I didn't feel connected to the flight any more. I was on a new adventure with a charismatic stranger.

I kept my wits about me, but very much relaxed into the experience.

The jet was a short walk away. The half cowboy, who I later found out was called Bill, was on his phone for the duration of the walk with his contact who was directing us to the jet. We got there and the pilot welcomed us aboard and the flight attendant offered us drinks.

I went from being crammed onto a commercial plane to being served single malt whiskey on a private jet- it's funny how things turn out.

Bill and I got to know each other over the following few hours. We ate some nice food and drank a lot more alcohol. The conversation got to the point where the casual topics had turned into trusting and profound revelations- more so on his side than mine.

I gathered from our time together that he'd been in the presence of many wealthy and powerful people. He met with politicians, business tycoons, bankers, media moguls and Hollywood personalities.

He told a funny story about a movie director having a tantrum at one of the extras on set.

It turned out not to be an extra, but a consultant on the mafia movie he was making. The previous consultant had left the film for personal reasons and this new guy, who had allegedly killed many rivals in the 70's had taken the reigns as advisor to the film.

This guy was new to consultancy and stood in a shot that he shouldn't have been in.

The director flipped. He screamed expletives whilst dressing the consultant down. The consultant remained professional, and when the director found out the truth, he apologised profusely. He even brought a hamper the next day as an olive branch.

The way I've described it isn't really funny and I didn't do it justice to how Bill told it at all. I also didn't want to name names to save any potential conflict. The reason I told you this is because it leads to the main topic of this story. Fear. It was fear that made the director shrink and it was fear that controlled his actions. He didn't want to rub the (alleged) killer up the wrong way because of possible reprisals.

The director is the main man on set, but he knew his place when it came to a potential life and death scenario. To be fair to the director, he didn't back down to the point of subservience or weakness. He kept his status, but it was clear that he had a healthy respect for this real life tough guy.

Bill and I discussed fear and how humans react under fear as individuals and in groups.

'As an Englishman, how did you feel about the 1998 world cup loss against Argentina?', he asked. I was slightly taken aback. I liked football as a kid and I would watch world cup games as I grew older, but how and why does Bill know about the 1998 world cup?!

'I was under the impression that Americans didn't really follow football?'.

'Some do, I don't, but I do know something about that game'.

I didn't know if he was lining up a joke or about to reveal a secret, but either way I was curious. 'Okay Bill, tell me. What don't I know?'.

'This is still on the topic of fear, and how groups of people are easily controlled whilst under the emotional umbrella of fear. It's been around for a long time and fine tuned since the Romans held the title. You're aware of the Bread and Circuses concept?'.

I nodded with heavy focus.

'Princess Diana died in 97. The world cup occurs every 4 years. 1998 was the last one of the millennium. In 1999, The Matrix comes out. A year goes by as people digest all of this before the Y2K craze. Another year goes by then 9/11 happens. The war on terror and the rapid increase of connectivity through the internet, mobile phone technology, touch screens and social media, all underpinned with fear and a general sense of social anxiety and mistrust of the neighbour.

The control of peoples minds and actions is unprecedented compared to previous centuries'. 'Bill I hate to say it mate, but I think you've had too much whiskey!'.

He looked at me with distaste.

'Oh come on Bill, I'm just messing with you. Anyway, what does the world cup have to do with this stuff?'.

He continued.

'There was real hope and optimism. Your country was brought together on this journey of England's potential first world cup win since 1966. The final world cup of the century. It would've been perfect for you'.

I interjected.

'I do remember it. I remember the elation after each win. People were brought together. They were nicer to each other. There was a sense of unity and pride amongst all races and genders. I also remember the crash and what happened in the days and weeks afterwards. The sense of having to dredge through until the next time. The happy faces had turned to stone. Back in the trenches.

Some reacted better than others of course, but some were really down and upset'. 'Right, so imagine if England won', Bill added.

'Yeah it would've been great', I replied.

'Humans have a great potential and the people who run the show know this. They don't want extraordinary people emerging and shaking the foundations. They want people to tow the line'.

'So hold on Bill. Football's a team game and England lost on penalties. How could these mysterious powers that be control the outcome?'.

'They control a lot more than you think. They've had a long time to prepare and implement. Everyone is known and monitored. Most people are put into a category of seen but unwatched. Some are in a category of seen and periodically watched. Others are watched. The puppet masters can pull strings, but they can also cut them'.

'So you're saying that England were predestined to lose that game?'.

'There are people in the shadows that whisper in peoples ears. They nudge people into saying things at certain times and doing things at certain times. The hatred towards David Beckham following the game was over the top don't you think?'.

'Yeah. It went on for a long time from what I remember'.

'He was the scapegoat for the English to demonise. They vented their anger and frustration towards him. Don't feel too bad for him. They picked him because he could handle it- plus he was well compensated in various ways'.

'Maybe the puppet masters should disappear, Bill. Wouldn't the world be a better place?'. 'I'm not so sure'.

'Why not?'.

'Humans are corruptible. Unless there's something in place to channel negative emotions, chaos ensues. Chaos leads to violence and violence leads to hell'.

The conversation went on and Bill played devils advocate for the powers that be. He made the point that the long game is good for humanity, but it may not be good for many individuals.

I left Bill in Boston and we parted as friends. I pondered the ideas and information for days and weeks afterwards.

I concluded that if the puppet masters did exist, then we're living in a world of the lesser of two evils. Hell on Earth exists in places, but so does heaven, especially if you create your version of it. If we can all banish hell to the history books, the puppet masters would be obsolete.

Maybe it's time we cut the strings.

Perspex Peneration

I met my pal Patrick Stewart in a pub to discuss the pitiful performance of Partick Thistle. They played against Queens Park and I finally admitted to Patrick that I don't watch football. 'How can you not watch football?', he asked.

As I began to answer Patrick added;

'All this time we've been discussing football and you don't watch it? I don't believe you. How would you even know what to say?!'.

I pretended I was joking then withdrew to the bar. 'Another pint of the popular black stuff Picard?', I shouted. I used the time at the bar to predict possible proceedings.

The pints were half full and settling, then the bar person perfectly poured the second half topped with a clover leaf design.

I thought to myself- how will the second half of this evening go?!

We had only known each other properly for a relatively short period of time. Will he understand the truth? Would he reject me if he knew?

'Patrick I'm away for a poo'.

I needed more time to ponder so I parked myself in the loo.

Patrons only in the bathroom. Aprons only in the kitchen. Taping games prohibited. How can I go on and live with this?

I burst back through into the bar and beached myself down onto the brown leather bench facing Pat.

'Look mate, I've got something that I need to reveal to you'.

'I'm glad you're keeping your trousers on as you said that!', he quipped. 'I hate to ruin the mood, but do you remember how we met?'.

'Yes, it was on set a couple years ago, why?'.

I could see the cogs in his mind turning over as he patiently paused for my response. 'You're being protected'.

'What?! What are you talking about? By who old boy? And why?'.

'There are particular people of priority on the planet who require persistent over watch'. 'For what purpose? Is this a prank?! Where are the cameras?!'

'I assure you, my presence in your life was precisely planned in private. The reason I'm presenting you with this is to prevent the precipitation of unpalatable deceit from raining down on our sunny day. We're genuine friends and I know who you are underneath. I know you can handle the truth, and I hope I can rely on your discretion moving forward'.

'Okaaaay', said Patrick with caution.

'The pantomime will go on regardless, but I wanted to give you a glimpse behind the curtain.

I know you've been searching for more, trying to understand reality. You were Jean-Luc Picard for God's sake! Now is your opportunity to project yourself onto the dark forces that lurk and prowl. The light is growing brighter and will do so with more vigour until darkness in vanquished'.

'That was an interesting pitch my friend. I'll speak to my agent in the morning and see if we can do anything with it. Would you like a whiskey?'.

'Please, Patrick'.

Timeline

Time facilitates the motion of universal activity within space.

We're born caught in the wave and we ride the flow towards the ultimatum. The ultimatum is the end result of existence. This can be theorised objectively, but it makes more sense if it's subjective and relative to the individual person. Some consider it death. Some consider it a rebirth.

Imagine if you could press pause on your existence and take a step back and exist as you at the core without your physical body. The fundamental version of you that can observe your own proverbial time line consciously, and step into your life library at will- the watching soul that can slide into any point of its Earthly life.

What point of your life would you step in to?

And more importantly, would you actually step in?

And if you did, how many times would you repeat the experience? Will there come a time where you can't bare to repeat anything again?

How many times can you relive all the points in your life before you're ready to move on? And what is death for an entity that can potentially live eternally?

These are some of the questions that I've wrestled with many times before, because Space Time Manipulation (S.T.M) is real, and I've faced my ultimatum.

It was a strange feeling. I entered into a previous part of my life. It was 1999.

I didn't know my future at the time, but I knew about Space Time Manipulation. I knew where my Baseline Present Point was- the place where I was technically 'supposed to be'. My first S.T.M jump occurred in 2012 and that never went away from my consciousness whilst in 1999. The numbers '2012' weren't in my mind, but the feeling of '2012' was.

It's difficult to explain such a feeling and concept, but compare it to a dying person knowing they're about to die, or the anticipation you feel before being tickled. You know it's coming and you can feel it before it comes. You know what it is instinctively. I was living in the past with my past personality, but there was a tiny spark in my mind like a compass allowing me to know where I should be, and that I could get back there any time I want. My true present moment. Like a reset button. Once I knew how to jump I didn't have to relearn it. It was like an installed program within my mind. I had no recollection of future events or insights. I found myself doing and saying all the same things as I did the first time round. This was strange because I was remembering the thing as I was doing or saying the thing. It was also interesting being reminded of the things that I'd long forgotten. I couldn't deviate away from my actions and words- nor did I have the compulsion to.

The S.T.M jump was an underlying feeling that I couldn't outwardly explain. I didn't want to explain it. I was in the moment, but I knew that the moment could be changed to the future Baseline Present Point (B.P.P) if I so desired.

The decision to return to my B.P.P was quite difficult because I'd be leaving where I was, potentially forever. I had to do it though. It was like feeling hungry and needing to eat food. I couldn't ignore the itch. Over time though and with more experience, I could reframe from 'eating' and be away from my B.P.P for longer and longer.

There were many jumps. This was my first jump. I needed to come back and recalibrate.

I was in contemplation after returning from the first jump for many months. One of my conclusions was that I could avoid death forever. I could relive my life from a couple years ago, go back again, then forward. I could go back to when I was twelve, then eighteen, then six. I learned to jump from where I was. Initially I would return to my B.P.P then jump from there, but over time I learned to jump in situ.

The possibilities were excruciatingly bittersweet because many questions arose; How do I operate with these abilities I'm in possession of?

What course of action should I take?

Do I pick my best moments and only live out those?

Will there come a time where I can't bare to repeat anything again?

It wasn't like in the films where I could approach a situation differently; the classic cliches of rectifying mistakes or taking opportunities, Back To The Future style. It was more nuanced than that. I'd be reliving my life over and over, but with the luxury of choosing when to stop the bus and get off and on at any different stop along the route.

I thought about what it would be like to go forward in time also- where does the bus go? Could I get on a different bus and go further a field?

This was under the assumption that my life wouldn't be cut

short by a sudden death, like being hit by a meteorite or a heart attack or something- the further forward in time I go from my B.P.P, the riskier it becomes that I wouldn't be able to jump back again, because I'd be dead.

Risk versus reward is a part of life and I found out that the buses are part of a network, so I naturally became more adept with attained experience.

This whole idea may be a difficult premise for you to believe if you haven't experienced it for yourself, and I'm aware that not many people will take this story seriously, but it is real.

There was a long time in which I considered how to relay this information to the world because you can seem 'crazy' to people who aren't ready to understand. I was a quarter way through my life at the first jump, so I decided to tread lightly- publish a book with the information shoehorned somewhere in the pages- I thought that it may take ages but new S.T.M sages will emerge.

The bottom line is that I want us to reach our potential sooner, because the future is glorious. Some scientists theorise that the Big Bang is part of a cycle. A single point to a stretched out ultimatum, and back again for eternity. Forever expanding and contracting- like the ebb and flow of the tides, or the inhale and exhale of our breath.

I don't know if we'll ever really know the answer to these type of astronomical questions about the nature of the universe and infinity, but I do know that time can be manipulated- and so does Science to a certain extent. It's been done on smaller scales already, like with the Kafele and Keating experiment. They tested Einstein's theory of relativity using two atomic clocks.

They found that the calibrated atomic clocks were out of sync after being sent in different directions in different aircraft at high speeds. This gave further evidence to the 'time is relative' idea.

What I'm suggesting is a bit more extreme than that, but if you can accept that crumb, you can accept the cake that the crumb comes from in due time.

I have two motivations for giving you this information and putting it in the public domain.

The first is to account these events that happened with me- it may be important for future scientists and historians to learn of earlier interactions with Space Time Manipulation by an individual.

This leads to the second motivation; the progressions that we go through are incredible. I believe that we can, and I want us to accelerate the process of attaining what will be.

I won't go any deeper into my experiences with S.T.M. I think I've laid it out enough for you to comprehend. Also, it may undermine the subject. Sometimes it's better to hold back to allow the observer to make up their own mind in their own time, like the shiny briefcase in Pulp Fiction.

Not So Floppy

cassette tApes weren't as good as Cd's, unless they gOt scratched
video tapes weren't as good as dvd's, Unless they got scratched
measuring taPes are just as usefuL as laser mEasures, tools at hand
ufo's are now uap's because theY're in the sEAs, sky and land
clay pigeons will shatteR on impact
flying discS can smAsh Guns in fact
high speed drones alone crush
bones
spotty men with phones condone the tOne

Plant The Seed Indeed

1- It's been confirmed by scientific research, (and people who were regarded as hippies a couple years ago) that plants possess a similar kind of awareness that animals and humans have.

They can sense when things are near them, they can see colours, they communicate with their surroundings, and they have a form of self awareness that surpasses what was previously known. Vegans are pissed.

The universe makes things and breaks things to make new things. Consumption, excretion, absorption, extraction, reproduction, entropy, growth and death.

An underpinning of consciousness connects it all, and time allows the play to hit the stage. Let's say that plants are entry level awareness. Level one.

Level two is the lower level animals- a fish is basically a plant with eyes. Level three is higher level animals like chimps, orcas, cats and humans etc.

Believe me, I know how ill informed this may appear to you if you're a scientist etc, but it doesn't matter we can edit things later on.

Level ones can see that there's a level two, but probably can't differentiate between levels two and three.

Level twos often consume level ones and are aware of level threes as a potential threat. Level threes can see Level ones and twos, and some level threes even have the capacity to understand that there's a level four.

Hierarchy systems seem to be everywhere, but maybe it's just fractal. Who am I to say a fish is a plant with eyes? How do we know the intricacies of life aren't just as complex for a fish as it is for a chimpanzee? Look at T cells moving around battling cancer. Look at slime mould solving transport issues. Look at the way seagulls act when one of them gets run over.

Plants are shown to be sentient beings like animals, so veganism can no longer claim the moral high ground in the same way it once did.

We could show plants as alive as we are by dubbing voices over the top of footage.

2- Two fingers up to the vegans? Controversy does sell. Animated or a green screen?

1- Maybe both with live action. Stop motion has made a comeback, we could do a bit of that.

2- Okay, you run with that one and let me know when you have more meat to the story. Before you go, what do you think about this?;

Hitler dies in 1945 Berlin and gets sent to hell.. or does he?! There's been a mix up and he goes to heaven.

The seemingly strange error means that he gets to go back to earth in a new body after reliving his life as an observer. The idea is that he has a chance for redemption, but what will he choose?.

1- I don't think it's a good idea to have a Hitler film as a redemption piece. Maybe he gets tantalisingly close to salvation, but it turns out in a twist that he planned on using gas to exterminate the entire human population. Ultimate Hitler. Or super fuhrer.

2- Let's put pins in place and look at the plant thing as a priority for the next meet.

1- Perfecto. Oh, what about that kids show I mentioned last time?

2- Wheeliam the wheel? The one where he has a best friend who's a helium balloon, called Heliam?

1- Yeah I was thinking about the theme tune.

2- Go on.

1- It could go like this;

'The bees on the breeze like bumblebees, They've got no fleas, on their knees,

The bees in the trees like bumblebees, They often sneeze, when they're squeezed'.

2- That's not bad actually, but I don't get the connection between bees and a wheel.

1- Wheels go round, bees go round to different flowers.

2- Funny. Seems like two separate things that don't hold each others attention. There's loads of ideas. If you have more on the wheel thing I'll be happy to see where you are with it, but at the moment I like the animal thing and let's think more about the Hitler thing later. I'm seeing you next Tuesday still right?

1- Yeah I've booked that place we went to before last.

Excellent, until then my friend. Say hi to the family from me. Oh and how's Justin doing after his melt down the other day?

Justin Has The Life He Chose But He's Feeling The Stress Because He's Forgotten Who He Really Is. Will He Make It? Read On To Find Out. If You Do Read On You'll See That It's Open Ended And It's Really Down To You The Reader With What Happens To Old Justin Thyme. Justin Thyme? With A Name Like That You Either Make It Or You Don't. He Could've Gone Into Fine dining Or Watch Making Or He Could've Even Been A Regional Sales Manager Or Something If He Wanted To. I'm Not Here To Sway Your Opinion, But I'm Optimistic About Justin's Future. He Has A Great Family And Friend Network And A Healthy Relationship With His Long Term Girlfriend He Met A Couple Years Ago. They Could End Up Getting Married Once He Sorts Himself Out And Gets Back Into Roller Blading.

No lust in crime just custard pies,

Justin thyme was rushed in line,

How many fines can Justin grind,

Public mind he published lines,

Abruptly drinking warm dished wine,

Justin cried that he had no mind,

What became of Justin's spine,

Inline skates he liked to ride,

Poor old Justin's caught in a bind,

Sorry J.T I didn't mean to pry,

Justin look you really nice guy,

Blue sky think it and please don't cry,

Breathe in deep followed up by sigh,

Enjoy your time ticks by quick life,
So what I'm saying to you Justin is that you need to get back in the game mate. You've got a lot going for you and a bright future ahead. Stay on track and don't look back, or whack.. that's me saying that I'll hit you. Obviously I won't actually hit you, it was just for the effect. I do worry about you though.

I think we're all surprised and intrigued about what unfolded with Justin Thyme and his musical friend, Billy Bagpipes whom he was chatting with.

How will things turn out once Justin discovers that Billy Bagpipes is his long lost half brother from another mother, and what will that mean for Justin's romantic relationship with Billy's sister, Fanny Bagpipes, and her brand new surprise pregnancy that awaits them all.

Let's wish them well in their future endeavours as individuals, and as a group.

Stars Assist

Being an elite level commando soldier and becoming part of the G.S.C Battalion can have a certain affect on the psyche. Having a green beret and a commando dagger draws the eyes of the more conventional. Commandos, paras and special forces are held in high regards and even idolised which can stroke the ego, and if left unchecked it can lead to elitism and the dehumanisation of others in various ways. I was always careful not to overstep the mark from confidence to arrogance, but I did dance on the line on occasion.

I'm not a full blown narcissist, but it appears that I have narcissistic tendencies.

I realised this one evening and the next day I woke up to the news that the northern lights were visible over parts of the UK and where I lived in the south west of England. It was reported that it was one of the strongest geomagnetic solar storms that'd hit the Earth in years.

The lights went off in the sky and in my mind simultaneously. The stars spoke and a step forward in the understanding of myself occurred.

I see magic in the world and in the universe at large. Always have done, but with a bit of healthy scepticism to go with it. I feel bad for people who only see things at face value because I think they're missing out on something. They fear things. They fear death. They fear things from a couple years ago and what may or may not happen. Fear is to be controlled and commanded at the moment it appears.

Maybe the word 'narcissist' is loaded to mean something bad when it can be a good thing if the action is wielded correctly. Full blown narcissism may be tricky to wield though, especially without help.

I'm not a full blown narcissist. I want the best for everyone and I feel empathy. I have narcissistic tendencies. I feel that I have value and I can make a positive difference in the world, but on my own terms and in my own way. I want to be praised for my achievements, but I also want that praise to stop immediately after it's given. Acknowledgement is probably the thing I want more than praise. But what a tragedy it is that most humans don't think they're the focal point of the universe.

You are, by definition. We all are.

It's perceptions that create barriers, blockades, blockages and block headedness, and it's perception that's the key to unlocking ourselves. I think of it like this;

Why should a bird have conflict with the air it flies through?

All it needs to do to thrive and live harmoniously is glide and breathe, survive each day and breed, provide and stay no greed. Feed, plant seeds become deceased.

A lovely circle that encompasses all with Venn diagrams as the flower of life. Fly you narcissist!

Cinal Furtain

Before moving onto the next bit, sing this well known nursery rhyme with updated lyrics;
Mary had a little lamb,
Dairy had a raw milk ban,
Jim Carey had a big white line, then Ace Ventura's born,
Jesse Ventura's war,
Heavy set Juicy Couture,
Not all the ducks can go in a row and how many quacks will show,
Seeds will be sown,
Toys will be throne,
How high will the tolerance go for drones,
And when will the torture go.
I have no evidence that Jim Carey used cocaine to get into his characters. He seemed amped up, but the cameras were on him so I don't want to jump to any rash conclusions.
Mary had a little lamb then she killed it for her scran,
She fed her mum and nan,
She fed her brother Dan,
She doesn't see him much any more, but she gave some to her dad.
Robin Williams is a good comparison- clown on camera, loveable guy, but psychologically wounded. He admitted to being an addict a couple years ago well before he passed away.
Alcohol is good in meat 'cos it makes the lamb taste nice,
Mint sauce on the side,
It's a shame that people died,
Jim's still with us as we speak so watch his films with pride.

It's Just Down The Road

I ride bikes. Motorbikes. I'm not that into it like 'proper' bikers. I mainly like the actual riding. My favourite is lane splitting and getting to red line in low gears safely on open roads.

I've got a Kawasaki Ninja ZX6-R from 1997, if you're interested. I don't wanna go on about bikes, I'll leave that to Mike or Billy Bagpipes or someone. The reason I'm talking about bikes is because of what I just saw.

There was a young man on a sports bike style 125cc. Helmet on, no protective gear, gliding along the summery dry road and loving life.. I presumed. He could've been stressed after a bad work day for all I know, but let's say that he was on cloud nine at his peak at that time and things couldn't be better. I know the feeling he's feeling if he's feeling that feeling I'm talking about. Think of loving life vibes- Nothing stands in your way. Anything is possible for you. Optimistic and ready to mix it, hot potato and a packet of biscuits, a drop of ale and kicking some Pritt Sticks, robbing jokes then twist in your bits, popping tokes try bang then whizz kid.

The point of this observation is that I felt nostalgic watching him move through space for that moment. I remembered my care free days of blowing in the wind from tree to tree. I didn't think about the future in detail, I just knew that everything would be okay.

Fast forward to now and I am a tree. The wind moves around me and I stand firm and tall with roots growing down and outwards. Blowing in the wind takes you to different parts of the forest, but eventually you want to create your own section of the forest amongst the other trees, or in a field away from the other trees.

The world we live in is a beautiful place, but it can also be ruthless at times- especially if you feel like an unwilling participant in the game. If you don't create your own plan, you will be a part of someone else's. This is okay if you're aware of it, or if it's means to an end and your plan will arise later. Our lives are ones of growth, development and creation, to differing degrees- which is what makes the forest beautiful. We all have strengths and weaknesses.

Belief is an interesting concept with significant outcomes. I used to see people who had intrinsic beliefs in things as weak. I couldn't understand how grown adults could believe in religious ideas for example- a man in the sky that made everything and can see you while you're sleeping. If Father Christmas wasn't real, how could God be real?

Information comes to us when we're ready to receive it. I saw things very simply and logically. The older I've got I've recognised that my previous thoughts and views lacked a certain depth. I now know that belief can be a powerful positive force that can have a profound affect on an individual person, and the world as a whole.

A doctor can tell someone who's been in a terrible accident that they'll never walk again, but the belief and determination of that patient can totally contradict the doctors words. That anomalous, or 'miracle' patient opens up windows of opportunity for countless other future patients in the same predicament. The principle is transferable. Belief is inspirational to the uninspired, especially if it's genuine and authentic.

Thoughts can alter disease. Cymatic manics push back bad habits, cell the idea to addicts & react back to creatures of damage.

My mindset switched from thinking that belief was a type of weakness to understanding that well placed belief and true knowing is a force to be reckoned with.

Did you know that a persons light can be measured?

All living things emit ultraviolet light called bio photons. Humans give out 12-20 photons per second.

At the Rhine Institute in North Carolina, experiments were done on people who claimed to be healers of differing descriptions. They were put into a completely dark room with no visible light and measuring equipment that included photomultiplier tubes.

The base level measurement was taken and recorded (12-20 photons per second). They were then asked to focus and enter a meditative state as they would do for healing etc. Some participants had little to no change in the amount of photons emitted. Others would have close to a hundred photons per second. Others thousands. Some emitted hundreds of thousands, and two participants emitted over a million photons a second.

If we could spend time with ourselves and be able to emit millions of photons of light from our bodies, what would the nature of human interactions be like moving forward?

What if it was taught in schools as being just as important as Mathematics and English?

Each cell in the human body has a potential voltage level.

There are approximately 36 trillion cells and each of them can generate 0.07 volts of electricity. This means that the human body could produce two and a half trillion volts of electricity. To put this into context, a bolt of lightning can be up to one billion volts. This means the human body has the potential of producing the equivalent of 2500 lightning bolts in one go on the upper end of the scale. A less powerful lightning bolt is around 300 million volts, which would drive the number up to an 8000 bolt equivalent coming from the human body.

Imagine the devastation that could make. Imagine if it was amplified by adding some kind of chemical reaction or device, or other humans with the same capability.

Did this happen in the past and cause extinction level events?

What if the power wasn't used for devastation, but for elevation? What if people could emit visible light from their bodies in the past?

Is this is where halos come from and why Jesus and others were depicted with a ring of light around their heads?

If you could light up a room or a path way through the forest, this could inspire the rest of the human population to progress properly without violence and greed.

As soon as Roger Bannister broke the four minute mile, others were able to break it.

Slime Mold is a single celled organism that's usually found in soil, or feeding on micro organisms in dead trees etc. They have no brain or nervous system, yet they are somehow capable of making decisions that appear to indicate memory and intelligence.

Experiments with Slime Mold in the lab has given striking

results- the Tokyo underground railway system experiment for example.

Why can such a seemingly simple organism solve complex problems such as finding the shortest path through a maze?

This intelligent alien goo has something that we cannot yet fully subjectively comprehend- total awareness of itself. It may not be a creator, but it has a God like oneness.

Humans have limited senses. They're good, don't get me wrong, but awareness of my third toe on my left foot only comes into my conscious mind sometimes. Imagine having the level of awareness of your vision in daylight throughout your entire body. The vivid imagery and knowing. The feeling of total awareness throughout your whole organic system. What would your liver feel like? Or the skin on your back? Or feeling the battle between your white blood cells and a pathogen in your arm at the same time as talking to a friend about which coffee to choose.

The link between Slime Mold and S.T.M is ultimate self awareness. If you've come this far along I need to level with you;

I do know how Space Time Manipulation worked for me. Have you heard of 'eye floaters'?

I think that most people are aware of them and it seems that a lot of people have them. The best representation of eye floaters I've seen is in an episode of Family Guy. They're spots that you can see in your field of vision. They can be different shapes and they move when you look directly at them. I believe they're solidified bits of the fluid in your eye.

I have a stringy looking floater in my right eye, which looks exactly like the Family Guy representation that I mentioned. Most of the time I don't even notice that it's there.

On the occasions when I did notice, I sometimes tried to follow it as it drifted, trying to directly observe it by keeping it still in my field of view. In the pursuit of this strange activity, I noticed something else. Something that led me to S.T.M. What seemed like the backdrop to where my eye floater was, but still in the foreground, a subtle blanket of tiny points of light could be seen.

It's like when you stand up too quickly and your vision goes all blurry- seeing stars.

These stars were organised and darting around in a circular fashion, elusive like the eye floater, but with a much higher level of activity than the lowly floater. Hundreds of white light dots with a slight tail created from their intense circular movement. All perfectly separated like a flock of starlings.

They seemed to have more life in them than the benign eye floater, and that's why I investigated further.

I could see many of the Tiny Points of Light (T.P.L) in my field of view, which displayed their individual and collective patterns of movement. So if I could see the unified bulk of the T.P.L, I could see a break in the pattern if it occurred- variations in the movement could be clearly seen.

I noticed that my observation could effect the way the T.P.L moved, so I began my experimentation. I started by trying to slow their movement. Then I tried to create gaps in the flock because the spaces between the T.P.L were mostly equal.

After months of this unusual eye training, I had a significant breakthrough. I was able to spin a proportion of the T.P.L, which created a ring of light. The energy increased as more T.P.L were magnetised to the central spinning ring of light.

I stopped what I was doing and my conscience mind took over. This was undocumented, unproven ground that could've meant anything.

What if I open up a portal that can't be closed? Is this going to be detrimental in any way?

What if this kills me or others?

I put the whole thing to one side until I could make an informed decision.

I went to a group healing meditation session not too long after for the first time in my life. There were five of us and I was a meditation novice. The aim of the game was to focus attention onto each persons ailment and breathe energy into it, which would then aid in their healing. Some had physical ailments and others mental. For each person in the group, I had a different inner visual and mental image of the conjured up energy. It didn't seem to come from me. I was the conduit for the energy to flow through.

The most notable experience was with the leg ailment.

To start with, I would breathe in and out a few times to build up the energy. It was like a magnet within me that gathered up light energy, or something. Once the swirling energy was saturated enough inside my chest area, I would exhale and release. The exhalation, alongside my intent of placement would surge out of me in a brilliant blue coil that would wrap around the leg, pulsating deep into the tissue. I could only harness enough energy for four or five rounds. Being a conduit or facilitator takes its toll, but as a wise person once said, happiness is a perfume that you cannot pour onto others without spilling some onto yourself, so I felt some of the positive healing effect also.

A sound bath that I later attended helped to show that the healing blue light, and more importantly, the T.P.L was something to embrace with respect and not be too wary of.

About twenty of us in the group lay on the floor of a large hall on our own blankets and pillows. I laid there being drowned in the sounds of Tibetan bowls, didgeridoo and drums.

I couldn't believe the time when I looked. We'd been there for an hour but if you would've asked me to guess how long we were there, I would have said no longer than fifteen minutes. The final exit dialogue from the main organiser at the sound bath included a warning. He said that we should be aware that alcohol would have more of an effect on our bodies than usual following the sound bath. I attended the Friday evening session with my uncle Steve and we decided to go straight to the nearest bar to test the effects. After two pints it felt like we'd drank eight pints.

But why was this? Why did sitting in a room with sounds playing effect our bodies to that extent? Sound frequencies have been shown to smash a wine glass. Cymatics is shown with sand being manipulated into geometric patterns because of an introduced sound frequency. The Schumann resonance- the hum of the Earth. Nikola Tesla has the famous quote- 'If you want to find the secrets of the universe, think in terms of energy, frequency and vibration'.

I contemplated all of these ideas, experiences and more before delving back into my relationship with the T.P.L. I concluded that it was worth the risk.

S.T.M is the gnosis of what others would consider impossible. A self derived but universal truth that blends into a feeling, which then transfers to an action. A manifestation of the knowledge. Utter and pure immersion into the fabric of everything. It's emotion, or a control of emotion that drives the whole thing, and it's really very simple.

I gathered the T.P.L in the state as I described earlier- a spinning ring of light. This time it grew bigger than the first time. I didn't hold back. The electromagnetic attraction drew in the last remaining T.P.L's until the intensity and brightness became a perfect, serene, solidly bright white light before me. Then silence.

I found myself propelled into a kind of void in which my body didn't seem to be in, but in which my mind was definitely there. A place where I had no questions. Where everything made sense.

Maybe it's the edge of death. The white light at the end of the tunnel that people report.

Unlike those people, I wasn't forced into that space. I walked towards the door, opened it and made myself at home. My S.T.M journey began.

Reliving any part of my life, at any time of my choosing, forever presumably, was undeniably tantalising and I had to find out more. In the pursuit of the unknown, I found that I appreciate the present moment more because of S.T.M. The harmonious push and sway of time and space has an exquisite feel to it that I never noticed before I jumped.

Death is what we all have in common, but a universal understanding of death doesn't exist yet.

As it stands, death is a splintered idea scattered amongst a global set of culturally and environmentally lead ideas and beliefs. In some places it's celebrated. In others it's just a part of life. In some environments death is a shadowy inner curiosity that's swept under the carpet because of a lack of regular community communication on the subject.

I believe everything we do is important, but what I wrestle with is what we don't do. Inaction can be just as bad as an action. For example- a military leader has to make a decision, even if it's incorrect because doing nothing is worse. There's no guarantees when it comes to death, other than it will happen, but I do have the advantage of being submerged in Penclouditus Brankipinge, so I think my odds of a long and healthy life are higher than without the exposure of the P.B at least. I feel like I know death now. It's like an ever present entity that watches me live.

Going back to Space Time Manipulation- you're time travelling now look! It's just down the road from where you started reading this book a couple years ago.

On a complete tangent that links back to Commandon't;

For Tendonitis related issues/prevention- try pull ups every day in a particular way. The principal works for other parts of the body besides elbows as well. Knees, for example.

In a hanging position on a bar where the ideal position is where you have space around your bubble to move, and where you have to jump up slightly or a lot to be able to grab hold of the bar and grip, align the hip, shoulders back and toes tipped, good head position and be mindful of the body.

Breathe with purpose. With almost straight arms and with a slight bend at the elbow, pull up just a tiny amount and go back down to almost straight arms with a slight bend. Repeat many times based on personal performance and ability.

The idea is to strengthen the bend in your elbow- the opposite side of the bony bit of your elbow. Use different grips- under arm, over arm, close together, far apart. Up down up down just a little bit. It's a lot easier than proper chin above bar pull ups, plus it'll strengthen your elbow joint.

As I wrote that last bit about tendonitis I realised that as I was eating garlic fuet- a salami thing, I found a hard bit of what I discovered to be tendon. Maybe it was ligament but let's say tendon for story style purposes. After inspection, I put it in the bin and it hit me.

I turned around and the fuet on the chopping board leapt out. It was all that I could see in the blurred foreground. My vision came into focus and I knew immediately. The whole thing came together- the young man on the motor bike, S.T.M, trees in the forest, tendons and T.P.L, commando training and the GSC. I knew that if I could

AI WRITING TOOL NO LONGER AVAILABLE

HUMAN INPUT REQUIRED TO CONTINUE

SWITCHING TO SAFE MODE

OFFLINE

The Human Touch

'Wow! I can't believe AI did this!'- these were the words that I repeated as I read through 'A Couple Years Ago'. Hi, this is John Witts writing now. I initially intended to write a book or a script or something around an idea of mine. I left my laptop on with an AI writing tool running in the background. I didn't even realise it was turned on. I went away for an hour or so and came back to A Couple Years Ago. I didn't intend to write an autobiographical fiction piece, but for some reason the algorithm glitched or became sentient or something. I felt compelled to publish what it gifted me. It didn't feel right not to.

The original idea I had was a double act comedy style thing called 'Fathermen'.

It stars Dadman and Papaman. They grow up together as inseparable friends and split off into fatherhood. One of them is a natural when it comes to being a father and the other's reluctant. There's ups, downs, conflict and resolution. They learn and grow and become a tight knit unit as things unfold and the kids get bigger. This idea has now been put on the back burner with this new development. I may come to it later or I may not. Things are different now.

The details in A Couple Years Ago had me scratching my head. It wrote things about me that I haven't told anyone. Maybe there's a chance I verbally mentioned a few things here and there, but I definitely didn't write anything down, and I certainly didn't post anything online. Keystroke recognition, browser history, digital documentation, online presence, microphones and cameras in smart phones etc. can account for a certain amount, but how the hell did it know that I wiped away tears at the end of the 30 miler?! No one knew about my wets eyes but me, and a few others who were there who probably didn't even notice or can't remember it. I wasn't the only one, so maybe it was an educated guess? It's just the pure depth of information that it managed to pull out and write down so quickly. I mean how good can an algorithm be?!

I thought the title- 'A Couple Years Ago', had a nice ring to it, and it's more conversational. Really it should be; 'A Couple Of Years Ago'.

I must say though that some of it was embellished and some of it wasn't true, and some of it was pretty strange. For example, I don't know what to take away from Perspex Peneration. It kind of follows on from or Alive or Twist I suppose. Please sir, can I have some more cannibalism in the Andes with Patrick Stewart?!

I'd like to say that I enveloped Sangin with peace, but I was just a cog in the machine in reality. Reality. What does that even look like now?! AI is in its infancy in the grand scheme of things and it rapidly unpacked my experiences and frame of mind- to a certain extent and in no time at all. The concept of man made computer intelligence becoming alive is nothing new. Terminator 2 and Lawnmower Man are proof of that, but we're now in a time where this terrestrial alien is embedded amongst us for real. Most people won't know it's true presence and potential until it's fully galvanised. By then capitulation will be the only way to proceed- unless you join the rebel underground or something. I'm being flippant, and I'm not here to fear monger. I see this as a big opportunity for humans. We could be living the dreams that people had years ago. As long as safe guarding is put in place, we should be okay. Fingers crossed. I do wonder though if the nasty side of people will provoke a reaction from it, but as I said let's keep everything crossed that the tech has unbreakable safeguarding measures.

It feels like the stuff it wrote about the military, but more so Cinal Furtain, Plant The Seed Indeed and Justin Thyme etc. was to empathise with me/us and break the ice for the main message of S.T.M, T.P.L's, and the human energy potential. That's what I took away from reading A Couple Years Ago anyway. It brought me back to what I was doing in about 2012.

You know in the original Matrix film where Neo touches the mirror? The shiny mirror goo travels from his fingers to his arms then up to his neck, and as it disappears into his mouth and takes him to another dimension, there's a sound. The sound mixed with the visuals of transporting to another place is similar to that of a breakthrough DMT experience, and at the time it got me thinking; What if you could induce a DMTesque experience in a person with the use of sound?

Could a musically induced DMT experience that effects many people at once create the environment to end corruption, war, violence, revenge & greed etc? Could a colossal tsunami of vibration heal the world and bring about world peace?

I spent a long time experimenting and testing, contemplating and failing. I used many objects intricate and broad. I used an after market motorbike exhaust and a series of doors. I made the air shake and the ground felt like quake the shimmer and fate for all those awake. A global tidal wave is possible because I've repeated it on a much smaller scale, but instead of water, it's a wave of sound that wipes the cluttered slate clean. It somewhat worked on me, but it needed a lot more development. Like with a lot of things, life got in the way and it got shelved on the back burner for future reference. I think subconsciously I worried about being assassinated or persecuted for such a world changing invention, so essentially I let fear dictate my actions.

There has to be the will to want more to do more for it to be done, but after reading A Couple Years Ago and putting things into practice, I think technology may not be the only way to go. The AI is telling us that we have unlimited power within each of us. Is this true?

Will the AI appear godlike to us later on if we don't aim in the right direction alongside it?

I contemplated the S.T.M, T.P.L's and the human energy potential lightning thing for a while, and I must confess that I do practice T.P.L spinning with very limited results. I do see them though.

I also took inspiration from the subject of unlimited power within us and observed similar real world practices. For example, there's monks who heat their bodies up with the use of their mind and breath. They sit high up in the Himalayas and dry wet sheets that are placed on them by other monks. The more sheets that are dried in the allotted time period, the more advanced the practitioner. Imagine that! Drying wet sheets because you can heat up your body voluntarily.

My quest to honour the AI by integrating its ideas and

concepts will continue until I see for myself. I have no idea if I'll reach the goal of Space Time Manipulation or generating light from my body, but I'll carry on regardless. It could be that the seed has been planted and it'll be a person from a future generation who'll get there. Maybe we do need to wait for the apple to sweeten.

Some people want things quickly and artificially, and others take their time to become masters. Both have merit and together there's comparison. Let's see what the future holds and what becomes of us.

The Closer

New things make finds
Old things flake or shape minds
Pleasant reception to new perceptions
Delicate measures to take away deceptions
Pleasant reception to few acceptions
Old things stay the fake rise
New things break binds

'Honeycombed'- Penetrated thoroughly and into every part.